D1372116

# IF IT WEREN'T FOR BENJAMIN

## (I'd Always Get to Lick the Icing Spoon)

*Story by* BARBARA SHOOK HAZEN

*Illustrated by* LAURA HARTMAN

**HUMAN SCIENCES PRESS**
72 Fifth Avenue
NEW YORK, NY 10011

*To my brother Charles—*
*with love and thanks*
*for teaching me all about*
*towhees, poker and icing bowls,*
*among other invaluable life lessons.*

Copyright © 1983 by
Human Sciences Press, Inc. 72 Fifth Avenue,
New York, N.Y. 10011
All rights reserved
Printed in the United States of America
1 98765432

**Library of Congress Cataloging in Publication Data**

Hazen, Barbara Shook:
  If it weren't for Benjamin I'd always get to
lick the icing spoon.

  SUMMARY: A young boy describes some of the
frustrations and advantages of being a younger
brother.
  [1. Brothers and sisters—Fiction] I.  Hartman, Laura.  II.  Title.
PZ7.H314975If          [Fic]          LC      78-26403
ISBN 0-87705-384-7
     0-89885-172-6 pbk.

If it weren't for Benjamin,
I'd always get to lick the icing spoon.

All the toys under the Christmas tree would be for me.

I'd never have to share, or take turns.

Benjamin's my brother.
He's bigger than I am
because he was born first.

What I want to be
is bigger than Benjamin.
But I never am.
I'm bigger than I was last year,
but I'm never bigger than Benjamin.

Benjamin has scissors with points.

He gets to stay up late
and go to the store,
because he can cross the street.

I wish I were Benjamin
so I could go to the store.
He says it's not such a big deal.
He says sometimes he'd rather play baseball.
He says sometimes he wishes he were me
because I get babied, and he gets stuck
with all the hard stuff.
I say I'll trade any day.

Mommy says, "Boys! Stop squabbling.
Be happy being yourselves."
    Sometimes it's hard.

I wish I were Benjamin
so I could jump higher,
and run faster,
and hit harder.

I keep trying to catch up.
I never do.
But I get closer.

And I can do some things
Benjamin can't do—
like whistle,
and wiggle my ears,
and make up songs.

If it weren't for Benjamin,
there wouldn't be anyone to bug me,
or break my crayons,
or boss me around,
or hog the bathroom.

If it weren't for Benjamin,
I wouldn't be in trouble all the time—
like the time I dropped the ant farm,
and all the ants got out,
and everyone got mad at me
and said it was my fault.

But it wasn't my fault.
It was Benjamin's fault
because he tripped me.

"It isn't fair," I said.
"Maybe not," said Mommy.
"It isn't possible
to be *exactly* fair ever.
I try to be as fair as I can."

When we play games,
Benjamin usually wins.

But not always.

When Benjamin has a friend over,
sometimes he closes the door,
and they won't let me play.
I used to cry,
and try to bang the door down.

Now I ask Mommy if I can have
someone my age over.
Or do something else that's fun.

Sometimes it seems like
everyone makes a big fuss
over what Benjamin does,
and nobody pays any attention to me.

Once Benjamin and I drew pictures
of the cat for Gramma's birthday.

She said Benjamin's picture was
"just wonderful."

She didn't even know mine *was* a cat!

I felt awful.

I was mad at everyone.

I felt like ripping up Benjamin's picture.
and mine, too.

Instead I went outside and kicked my ball.

When Gramma came out, she said
she didn't mean to hurt my feelings.

"Benjamin *is* good at making pictures," she said,
"the way you are good at making up songs.
You are each good at different things.
And you are both very special to me."

Then she gave me a cookie and asked
if I would make up a birthday song for her.

I felt a lot better.

Sometimes it seems like
Benjamin gets to do more than I do.
Last week Daddy took Benjamin
to a double-header.
He didn't take me.

I told Daddy, "You don't love me
the same as Benjamin."

"I don't love you *exactly* the same,"
said Daddy,
"Because you're *not* the same.

"But I love you every bit as much."

"Benjamin likes baseball.
That's why I take Benjamin
to baseball games.
You like animals and music.
That's why I take you
to shows and to the zoo."

I like it when Daddy takes me places—
just the two of us.

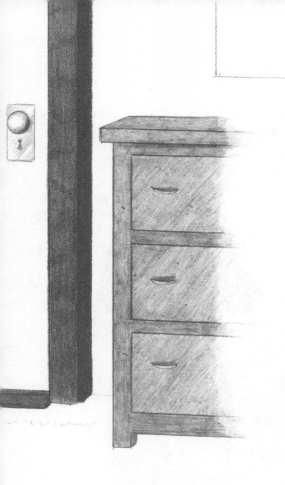

One day I asked Mommy,
"Who do you love better?
Me, or Benjamin?"
    "I don't love one of you better,"
said Mommy. "I love you both.
    "I love you for being you,
and Benjamin for being Benjamin.
    "I love you for what you are.
And I love you a bundle!"

    "Even when I'm naughty,
and Benjamin isn't?" I asked Mommy.
"Even when you're mad at me?"
    "No matter what you do
or how mad I am," said Mommy.
"I love you now, and always will.
Parents' love is like that."

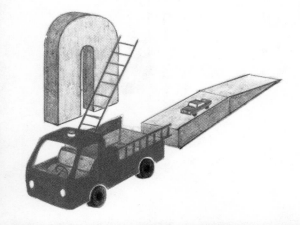

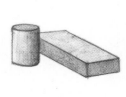

"I don't feel that way about Benjamin,"
I tell Mommy. "Sometimes I hate him
and wish he'd go away for good."

Mommy explains, "It's different
between brothers. And sisters.
And brothers and sisters. I felt the same way
when I was your age."

She said it's okay to feel that way,
and talking about it helps—
but no hitting and no hurting.

I'm glad we talked.

At night in bed I think,
if it weren't for Benjamin,
I might get lonely.

Who'd tell me jokes,
and help me fix my wagon,
and pull me up the sledding hill,
and walk between me and Bert the bully,
and show me how to bunt,
and say "That's it!" when I make a hit.

I think of the times we have fun together.

Funny how you can hate someone sometimes
and other times be glad he's your brother.

# Selected Children's Books

Barbara Shook Hazen
**VERY SHY**
Illustrated by Shirley Chan

Barbara Shook Hazen
**IT'S A SHAME
ABOUT THE RAIN**
The Bright Side of
Disappointment
Illustrated by Bernadette Simmons

Susan Kempler ; Doreen Rappaport; and
Michele Spirn
**A MAN CAN BE...**
Photographs by Russell Dian

Doreen Rappaport
**"BUT SHE'S STILL MY
GRANDMA!"**
Illustrated by Bernadette Simmons

Alfred T. Stefanik , M.A.
**COPYCAT SAM**
Developing Ties with a Special
Child
Illustrated by Laura Huff

Barbara Jean Menzel
**WOULD YOU RATHER?**
Illustrated by Sumishta Brahm

Althea J. Horner , Ph.D.
**LITTLE BIG GIRL**
Illustrated by Patricia Rosamilia

Jo Beaudry and Lynne Ketchum
**CARLA GOES TO COURT**
Illustrated with Photographs by
Jack Hamilton

Linda Berman , M.A.
**THE GOODBYE
PAINTING**
Illustrated by Mark Hannon

Corinne Bergstrom
**LOSING YOUR BEST
FRIEND**
Illustrated by Patricia Rosamilia

Cilla Sheehan , M.A.C.P.
**THE COLORS THAT
I AM**
Illustrated by Glen Elliott

Polly Greenberg
**I KNOW I'M MYSELF
BECAUSE...**
Illustrated by Jennifer Barrett

*Complete Children's Catalog available upon request*

**HUMAN SCIENCES PRESS, INC.**
**72 FIFTH AVENUE**
**NEW YORK, N.Y. 10011**